For Richard.

who loves the backyard as much as I do!

BACKYARD BEASTIES

Helen Milroy

 FREMANTLE PRESS

Chicken clucks

to greet the dawn

as possum

slips

across the lawn

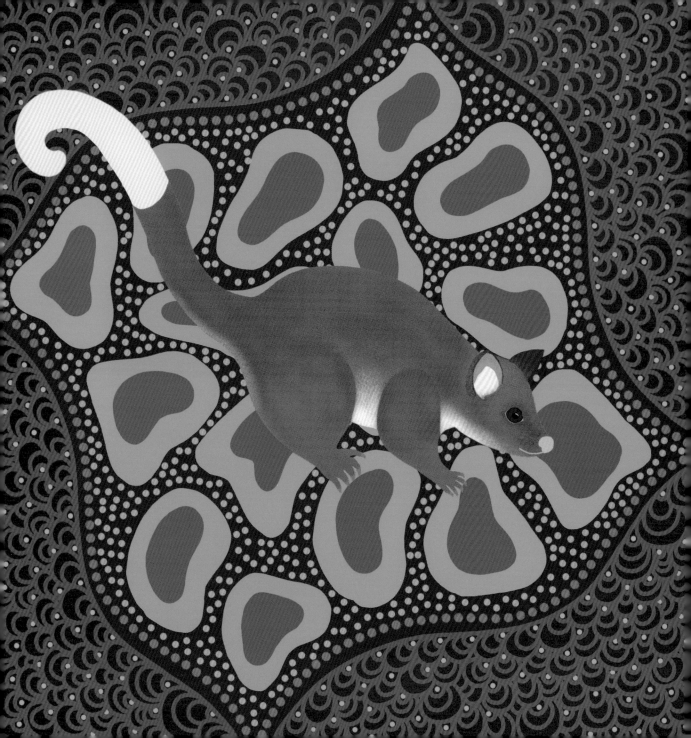

bobtail

ventures

slowly out

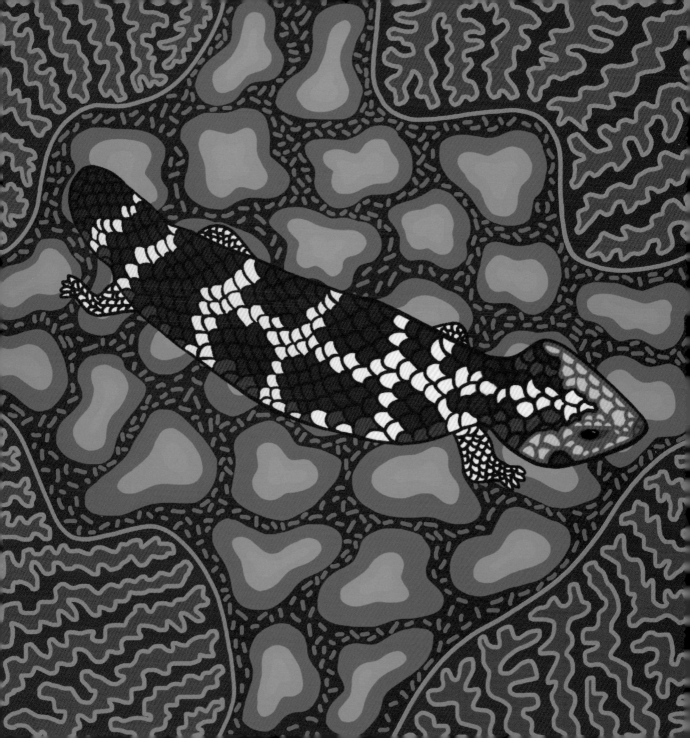

while **dog**

bounds

madly all about

turtle

slips

into the pond

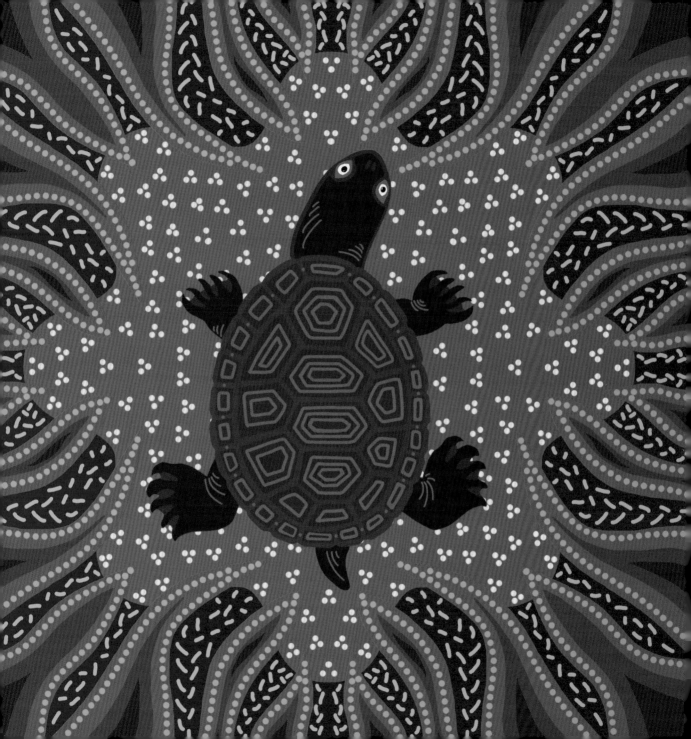

where gecko **lies**
beneath a frond

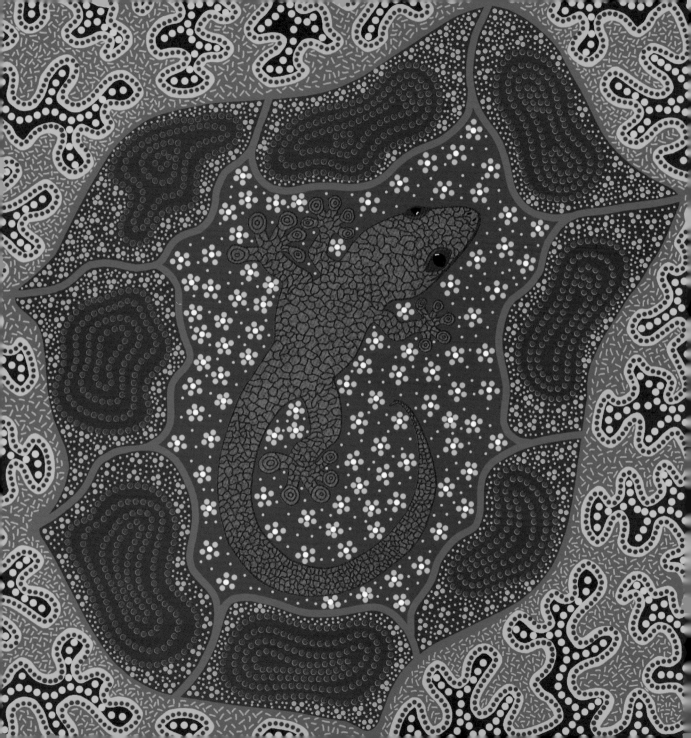

bat hangs
sleeping through the day

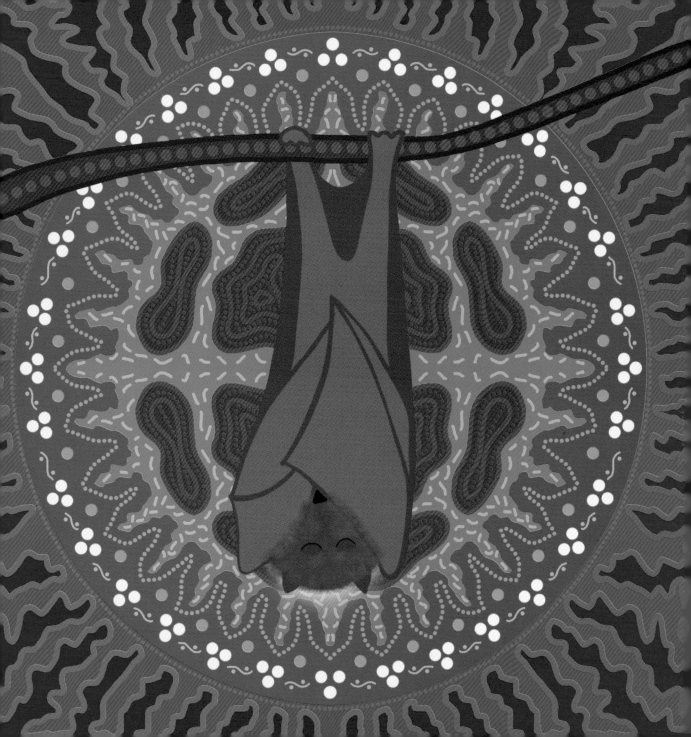

quenda, too, rests

hidden away ᶻ ᶻ ᶻᶻ

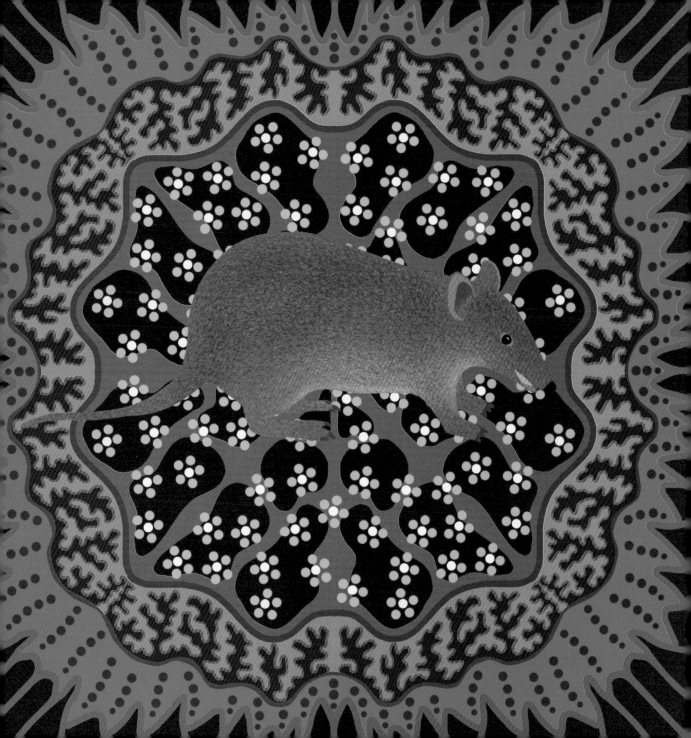

frog **croaks**

out a song of night

then cat begins a
!# noisy fight #/

Backyard beasties
all around.

With many more
still to be found!

Helen Milroy is a descendant of the Palyku people of the Pilbara
region of Western Australia. She was born and educated in Perth.
Helen has always had a passionate interest in health and wellbeing,
especially for children. Helen studied medicine at the University of
Western Australia. She is currently a professor at UWA,
Consultant Child and Adolescent Psychiatrist, Commissioner
with the National Mental Health Commission and the
AFL's first Indigenous Commissioner.

First published 2022 by
FREMANTLE PRESS

Fremantle Press Inc. trading as Fremantle Press
25 Quarry Street, Fremantle WA 6160
www.fremantlepress.com.au

Illustration medium: freehand digital artwork.
Designed by Rebecca Mills.
Printed by Everbest Investment Printing Limited, China.

NATIONAL
LIBRARY
OF AUSTRALIA

ISBN: 9781760991203

Fremantle Press is supported by the State Government through the Department of Local Government, Sport and Cultural Industries.

GOVERNMENT OF
WESTERN AUSTRALIA

Department of
Local Government, Sport
and Cultural Industries

lotterywest
supported